WINDOWS OF GOLD

and other stories

Also by Marianne Mitchell

The Ghost in the Wood
The Ghost in the Convent
The Secret Santa Suit
Finding Zola
Firebug
Joe Cinders
Maya Moon

WINDOWS OF GOLD
and other stories

by
Marianne Mitchell

Illustrations by
Agy Wilson

RAFTER FIVE PRESS

Printed in the United States of America by Createspace

Cover illustration by GraphicsRF/Shutterstock
Interior illustrations by Agy Wilson and Shutterstock

Published by Rafter Five Press
Tucson, Arizona

Summary: A collection of short stories for young readers.

ISBN: 978-1484188026
Library of Congress Control Number:2006908875
Second print edition

With special thanks:

To my first teachers,
Paula Nelson and Marion Moore.
They celebrated creative thinking and
always expected the best from their students.

To Kent L. Brown, Jr.
for his continued support of my writing.

To Jim for everything.
MM

To my wonderful family
Tom, Gabby and Dominique
AW

CONTENTS

WINDOWS OF GOLD

An American folktale

Nestled in the hills above a valley, there once lived a poor farmer and his daughter, Emma. Each morning as Emma lugged her milk pail and stool out to their old cow, she looked across to the other hillside and sighed. Each morning she saw the same beautiful sight. Far across the valley, golden windows winked back at her.

"Who lives in such beauty?" Emma wondered. "Who can be so rich that even their windows are made of gold?"

As Emma went about her milking, she thought about life "over there." Surely those people didn't have to get up early and do farm chores. They probably had dozens of servants cleaning the floors and polishing the windows. Every meal must be a banquet, not the simple stews and plain bread Emma and her father had to eat. Life in such a place must be spent having grand parties. It surely wouldn't be spent digging and hoeing, trying to grow potatoes in stony fields.

One day Emma's father said, "You look sad. What is the matter?"

"I wish we were rich," Emma answered. "Why do some people have so much and we have so little?"

"I have you and you have me. I think that makes us quite rich."

Emma sighed. "Have you ever been across the valley, Father?"

"No, I am happy here. Aren't you?"

"I want to see the palace with golden windows. I want to find out who lives over there," Emma begged.

Emma's father thought for a moment. "All right," he said. "But you must promise to be satisfied with what you learn."

Early the next day, Emma and her father hiked down the rocky hills and into the valley. By noon they had started the steep climb up the other side. Now and then they passed a small cottage,

Much too soon for my liking, I am back at home. Staring at the rust-colored door that leads back into my old life. Wondering if this is a good idea after all.

Balancing the luggage on one side, I struggle to unlock the door without losing my balance. What I see and hear when I finally get the door open throws me completely off guard.

Melodic sounds of smooth jazz and the flickers of several candles greet me as I enter the front room. Marcus is perched on the couch with his freshly shaved head laid back – the seeming picture of relaxation. Except for his weight loss, he looks much like he did before everything started. It used to be routine for him to come home from work and put on soft music to unwind. From time to time, we'd sit together for an hour or more without saying a word. Just being and enjoying a moment.

It only takes that little bit of nostalgia to melt all the grief and anger that has been mounting inside me. I start to pray that maybe, just maybe, the man I knew is still here . . . somewhere.

"Hey, sweetie . . . I'm back," I say tentatively. I take a few steps farther into the room and try to figure out what to say next.

"I . . . uh . . . well, I missed you." I don't care how weak it sounds. Even after everything we've been through, I still love him more than anything.

There is a brief pause during which I wonder if he heard me. But before I can repeat myself, he speaks.

"Hello, Angela."

It is a voice I don't recognize. Not one of anger, but certainly not excitement to mirror my own emotions. It is then that I notice his eyes. Still the same soft brown pools that I used to dive into, but now they look vacant and cold. Not like I remember. Before.

I am not sure what to say next, but decide that actions speak louder than words. I begin to move toward him, hesitantly, for fear of how he might respond.

40

'VE BEEN SITTING IN THE SAME SPOT ON THE EDGE
of the bed in Lela's guest room for at least an hour — since
Lela and Derek left for Wednesday night church service. The
room is completely dark, save the light that filters in under the
closed door, and the house is so quiet that I feel as if I can't help
but to hear myself think. That's when I hear the voice I've come
to know and trust.

It's time for you to go home.

Though I'd rather go almost anywhere else, after a few
weeks of hiding, I know the voice is right. I've been running too
long: Time to face my life, and deal with the madness instead
of waiting for it to magically disappear.

Although I have absolutely no clue what I'll do when I get
there, I quickly pack my belongings, moving swiftly for fear that
if I hesitate, I might change my mind. I really don't want to go.

After so much time away from home, I expected to have a
plan. But I don't. All I know is that it's time.

I take a few minutes to write a thoughtful note of gratitude
to Lela and Derek for opening their home, and place it on the
breakfast table. Then I throw my bags into the back of the
truck and hop in.

but their eyes were fixed on the hills above.

By late afternoon they arrived at a cluster of houses. All had thatched roofs and mud walls, just like their own. The fields around them were lumpy with stones, just like their own.

Emma saw a girl leading a cow out of a barn. "Good afternoon!" Emma called. "We're looking for the palace. Is it far from here?"

The girl stared at them, confused. "A palace? Around here?"

"Yes. The one with the golden windows," said Emma. "I know it has to be close. You see, we live over there, across the valley. Every morning I can see the golden windows from my yard."

The girl gasped, her hands flying to her mouth. "You come from over there?" she asked. "I have always wondered what your life must be like. Each afternoon I come out and marvel at your golden windows."

Emma laughed. "We don't have golden windows."

"Yes, you do! Look!" The girl pointed across the valley toward Emma's house.

Emma and her father turned and looked. In the glow of the afternoon sun, the windows of all the little houses on their side of the valley glittered like gold.

"I hope you can stay for dinner," said the girl. "It's not much—just a simple stew and plain bread."

Emma squeezed her father's hand, letting him know she was happy with what she had learned. "Thank you," she told the girl. "That sounds perfect."

CACTUS COYOTE

One bright summer morning, Coyote trotted down a dusty arroyo. As usual, he was hungry. He'd been out all night hunting for his dinner and all he had found were a few tiny mice. At last, his sharp eyes saw Rabbit dozing under some dry tumbleweeds. His swift paws caught Rabbit by surprise.

But Rabbit didn't panic. He poked his small fuzzy head out from under Coyote's paws and said, "Mr. Coyote, a great hunter like you deserves a bigger meal than me. I am much too small. Let me go and I will lead you to my brother's house. He is much fatter."

Coyote looked at the scrawny rabbit in his paws. *One rabbit is good, but two rabbits would be better*, he thought greedily.

"You're right," he said. "You would hardly be a mouthful and I am very hungry this morning." He put Rabbit down and gave him a shove. "Off you go, then. But no tricks! I am right behind you."

Rabbit scampered across the desert to the big paloverde tree where his brother had a cozy burrow. He jumped in and shouted, "Coyote is coming! We must hide!" So the two rabbits wiggled their way to a deep, dark corner.

This little trick wasn't going to stop Coyote. He knew all about rabbit holes. He looked around until he found the escape hole and he pushed a rock over it. Then he started digging. Soon his big, dirty snout was poking the two frightened rabbits.

"Finally, I can have my dinner!" growled Coyote.

And he ran a long, greedy tongue over his pointy teeth.

But Rabbit was very brave. He raised his paw and said. "Wait, Mr. Coyote! You have worked very hard today. You must be even hungrier now. Let us go and we'll lead you to our brother's house. He has spent all month eating juicy red cactus pears. He is much fatter than we are."

Coyote rubbed his stomach. A three-rabbit stew sounded even better than a two-rabbit stew. He backed away from the two rabbits.

"Off you go, then," said Coyote. "But no tricks! I am right behind you."

The two rabbits zipped through the sagebrush to the home of their big brother. He lived in a hole at the base of a prickly pear cactus.

"Coyote is coming! And he wants a fat rabbit for dinner!" they cried.

"And he shall have one," said their big brother. "Come. We'll fix up a surprise for him."

Near the prickly pear cactus grew another cactus called Teddy Bear cholla. It looked soft and cuddly but it wasn't. It had long, sharp thorns with little hooks on the ends. Chunks of cholla lay scattered all over the ground. The three rabbits gently pushed the pieces of cholla together until they had shaped a huge cactus rabbit.

Coyote arrived and circled around slowly. He peered into the huge prickly pear cactus, looking for the three rabbits. There were in there, all right. And sitting right next to them was the biggest rabbit he had ever seen.

"Holy guacamole," whispered Coyote. "What a delicious stew this will be!"

He quickly gathered up sticks to make his cook fire. Soon the flames were jumping. The spicy smell of mesquite filled the air.

"Come out, my friends, and sit by my fire. Let me tell you about my adventures."

But the three rabbits stayed where they were.

Coyote's stomach growled. The rabbits huddled closer together.

"Don't be afraid. That's just the sound of distant thunder," said Coyote. He tossed some more sticks on the crackling fire and the smoke billowed up.

The rabbits put their heads together and on the count of ONE. . . TWO. . . THREE! they blew the smoke into Coyote's eyes.

While Coyote sputtered and coughed and rubbed his eyes, the three rabbits dashed away into the desert.

Coyote looked into the cactus again. Three of the rabbits were gone, for sure. But . . . could it be? The biggest rabbit of all was still there!

"No more tricks!" cried Coyote. "Now you're mine!" He was so greedy and so hungry, he forgot to be careful. He clamped his paws around the cholla cactus rabbit.

"Ow-chihuahua!" Hundreds of spiky thorns pricked Coyote's paws. He kicked and danced. He tried shaking off the cholla. He snapped and chomped. "Ow! Ow!" From his whiskery nose to his long bushy tail, he was covered in cactus.

Coyote forgot all about rabbit stew. He limped down to the river to soak his poor stickery body. Why couldn't he learn not to be so greedy?

Safe and sound in their new burrow, Rabbit and his brothers sat down to a delicious dinner of prickly pear salad.

"Here's to the little guys!" they cheered.

And off in the distance they heard Coyote crying about his sore body and his lost dinner.

CAPTAIN PURPLE

"Hey, guess what! It's back!" announced Amy, coming in from the porch.

"What's back, dear?" asked her mother.

"Our garbage can—the one that blew away in the storm last week."

"Good. I was about to buy a new one," said Mom as she tucked peanut-butter sandwiches into two lunch bags.

"But how did it get here?" asked Amy. "Who brought it?"

"Don't have clue," said her older brother,

Morgan. "I had my paper route this morning, but I didn't see any suspicious characters carrying garbage cans."

"And I found these, too. What do you think it means?" Amy held up a paper cutout of purple footprints.

"You and your questions!" huffed Morgan. "It's just a prankster," he said, downing the last of his cereal.

"Pranksters don't return lost things," Amy said. "They do stuff like wrap toilet paper on the trees, the way you and your crazy friends do sometimes."

Mom picked up the purple footprints and read the message scrawled in black ink: Greetings from Captain Purple. "You know, we're not the only ones to get this message. Mrs. Castro over on Linden Lane got one last week."

"Did she lose a garbage can, too?" asked Amy.

"No. She told me someone replaced the burned-out light on her porch. They left the old bulb on the ground, next to a pair of purple footprints like these."

"A mystery! We should investigate, Morgan," said Amy.

"Sorry, not today, kiddo. I've got soccer practice, remember?"

That day at school, Amy quizzed her friends about Captain Purple. No one knew anything. During recess, she made a list:

EVENTS:

garbage can returned

light bulb replaced

CLUES:

purple footprints

SUSPECTS:

????????

It has to be someone who can get around town without drawing attention, she thought. Maybe it's a mail carrier or a police officer.

She added 'garbage collector' to the list of SUSPECTS.

After school she rode her bike over to Mrs. Castro's house. She felt sure she could pick up some more clues.

As they sat on the front porch sipping sodas,

Amy showed Mrs. Castro her list of clues and suspects.

"No, I don't think it was the garbage collector who fixed my light," said Mrs. Castro shaking her head. "That was a Wednesday. My garbage is picked up on Saturday."

"Could it have been your neighbor?" asked Amy.

"No, he's gone for a month to visit his grandson. Why don't you talk to Moses Jenks at the hardware store? He got some of those purple footprint things, too."

"He did? What for?"

"He lost his wallet in the park. It came to him in the mail."

"I knew it!" Amy added 'mail carrier' to her list of suspects. She thanked Mrs. Castro for the soda and pedaled fast to the hardware store.

But Mr. Jenks nixed her idea about the mail carrier. "It didn't come in the real mail," he told her. "It fell through the mail slot all right, but the envelope had no postage. Just my wallet—with everything there—and those goofy footprints."

"Could a police officer have dropped it off?"

Mr. Jenks laughed. "I don't think so. I know both of the officers who patrol this area. I can't imagine either of them pretending to be Captain Purple. Why don't you go talk to Mrs. Tanaka? I heard she got some footprints, too."

Amy thanked Mr. Jenks and hurried to the Tanaka house.

"Yes, we got some of these footprints last week," said Mrs. Tanaka. My son Winston's bicycle was in the front yard with a flat tire. He was waiting for me to fix it. Then one morning when we woke up, the tire had been fixed and we found the purple footprints beside the bike."

"Any idea who it could have been?" asked Amy.

"No, but it was a very nice thing to do. Winston was so excited to be able to ride his bike again."

Amy said goodbye and pedaled slowly toward home, trying to sort out the mystery. She stopped by the park where Morgan and his team were playing soccer.

She pulled out her list and added the bike tire to her list of events. On the back of the list, she sketched a map showing all the places where Captain Purple had struck. A pattern seemed to be taking shape.

"I think I know," she muttered to herself. "But I need proof."

When she got home, she found a note from Mom asking her to fold the laundry from the dryer. Usually Amy hated that job because it seemed so boring. But today she didn't mind. It gave her time to think. As she started sorting clothes, she groaned. Someone had left a tissue, or something, in a pocket. Purplish lint covered everything.

"Oh...!" gasped Amy.

Later, Amy poked her head into Morgan's room.

"Guess what?" she asked.

"What?" replied Morgan.

"I know who Captain Purple is."

"Yeah, who?"

"You!"

"Get real," Morgan snorted. "How could I be Captain Purple? I'm way too busy to—"

"You're busy all right. Your paper route takes

you right to Mrs. Castro's house where you could stop and change her light bulb. And by the Tanakas' where you could easily stop and fix Winston's bike tire. And your soccer practice is in the park where Mr. Jenks lost his wallet. Oh yeah, and the garbage can isn't our old one. I checked. It's a brand new one. It still has the price sticker on it."

Morgan waved her off. "Yeah, well that's an interesting theory. But you don't have any proof."

"Really? What about this?" Amy held out the purple lint and a crumpled piece of paper. "I found some of this purple stuff in your jeans' pocket. Plus, this little paper is a receipt for the new garbage can."

Morgan stared guiltily at the evidence. "Oh."

"These are nice things you're doing, Morgan. Why the big secret?"

"It's more fun this way," he said. "Nobody appreciated those pranks I used to pull. When they saw their trees decorated with toilet paper, they just got mad. Now, as Captain Purple, I get to sneak around and do good things. Promise you'll keep it a secret."

"I will on one condition," said Amy.

"What's that?"

"I get to join you as—Sergeant Scarlett!"

"Deal!" Morgan held out his hand. "You can start tomorrow. There's a lot of trash in the bushes along side the Anderson's house."

Amy shook his hand. "I'm on the case, Captain!"

EMERGENCY PILOT

Chris peered out the window of his dad's Cessna 172. Down below, the dry washes that cut across the Navajo reservation raced by under the wings. Here and there, a cluster of scrub pine broke the flat landscape.

Chris liked flying. He hoped someday he could take lessons. For now, he was happy being the navigator, checking their progress on an air chart. He had already located Humphries Peak on the map. Out the window the mountain loomed darkly against the setting sun.

"Glad you came along today," said his dad. "You can see how flying is the only way I get supplies to some of the ranchers out here." He added power and the small plane climbed some more.

"We're not the only ones flying up here, Dad. We have a stowaway." He waved his chart at the insect and missed. A few seconds later, it buzzed by again.

"Ow! Dad slapped his cheek hard. "Whatever it was, it just stung me."

Chris glanced down at his dad's lap. "It was a bee," he said.

"Rats! Let's hope it doesn't bother me," Dad said. "Flagstaff airport is about forty minutes away." He checked the instrument panel in front of him.

Chris did the same. A chill ran up his spine. He remembered that the last time his father was stung by a bee, his hand and wrist had become badly swollen. Chris wondered if the swelling would happen again. If it did, would he have to fly the plane? The only "flying" he'd done was on a computer, playing with the flight simulator.

They flew for a while in silence. Chris's mind filled with worry. The sunset on the horizon was fading fast. It would be dark when they reached the airport. He looked over at Dad's face. An angry red welt had formed just under his right eye. An allergic reaction was definitely beginning. Chris wished he could find some ice for his dad.

Dad winced with pain. The plane inched upward in the clear sky.

"What's the matter?" asked Chris.

"It's no good," Dad moaned. "I can barely see. I feel. . .woozy. We have no choice. You'll have to take over for me."

"But I can't fly a plane. Not for real!" Fear spread over Chris like an icy wave.

"I'll tell you what to do. You'll be my eyes and hands." Dad turned and gave him a pained smile. "I know you can do this."

Chris saw how swollen his dad's face was. He was about to get his first—and maybe his last— flying lesson.

"We're flying straight and level now," Dad said, his voice steady and reassuring. "Our heading is good. Do everything smooth and easy. No jerky movements, OK?"

Chris took hold of the yoke on his own side. This acted as the steering wheel of the plane. He scanned the instrument panel. He was grateful it was the same setup as on his computer simulator. At least he knew what the dials meant.

He looked over at his dad and was shocked to see how fast the swelling had spread. Dad couldn't even open his eyes.

"Keep the speed between seventy and ninety knots," Dad said wearily. "Can you see the city lights yet?"

"Yes," answered. Chris. Down below, the lights along Route 66 looked like a diamond necklace.

"Good. Find the university dome. It's a good landmark. Aim for that."

Chris's stomach churned. He had to fight the fear chewing him up inside. Concentrate on getting down safely, he told himself. His dad squirmed in his seat, trying to get comfortable.

Chris checked the instruments again. Airspeed eighty knots. Good. Altitude, ten thousand feet. Good.

Chris called the airport tower on the radio.

No answer.

He tried again. Still nothing.

"The tower must be closed," said Dad. His voice was getting weaker.

Chris let a nervous sob bubble out. "Stay cool, stay cool," he murmured to himself.

"When you see the dome, make a nice easy left turn. We want to come in on runway twenty-one. Don't worry about putting the wheels down. They're always down on this plane. Set the radio at 120.0. Maybe someone will hear you."

Chris turned the radio dial and tried again. "This is Chris Michaels. I'm flying my dad's Cessna. He's very sick from a bee sting. I'm trying to land in Flagstaff on runway twenty-one. Send an ambulance."

He listened for a reply. No response.

The lights of the university dome came into view on the left. It looked like a giant ice-cream sundae with a red cherry on top. Chris started his slow turn and decreased power. The plane began losing altitude for the landing.

When he straightened out, all he could see ahead was darkness. Panic crept into his voice as he asked, "Where's the airport? Where are the lights?"

"Click your microphone button three times," advised Dad. "It's automatic."

He clicked and like magic, the runway lights flashed on.

"Wow!" He checked his airspeed and decided to pull back on the yoke. Suddenly, the plane shook violently. An alarm bell blared in the cockpit.

Dad sat up. "It's a stall! Apply power, nose down, now!"

Chris's heart raced as he pushed the yoke gently forward. The alarm shut off. The vibrating stopped. He was in control again. The plane continued a normal descent. The altimeter clicked down by one hundred-foot intervals. The runway looked invitingly close. Pine trees swished by underneath.

"Bring the nose up a bit just before you land," said Dad.

They cleared the edge of the field. The wheels thunked the pavement as the plane bounced down hard and up again. It bounced one more time, then stayed down. Chris stepped on the foot pedals, braking steadily. Finally, they rolled to a stop. Ambulance lights flashed through the darkness. Someone had heard his call for help.

Chris slumped in his seat. "We made it!"

"Never a doubt," said Dad through a puffy grin.

THE KIDNAPPED PUMPKINS

"Aren't they the most beautiful orange babies you ever saw, Grandpa?" Ten-year-old Carmen poked her dirt-covered hands into her pockets.

"Yep, sure are. Best ever," said Grandpa.

As Carmen walked around her garden, dried leaves crunched like cornflakes under her feet. Soon it would be Halloween and she would have to cut her pumpkins from the vines and take them to the market.

Carmen and her grandfather had a small plot of land in the city's community garden lot. Here they had grown beans, tomatoes, squash, and beets. Now, as chilly weather arrived, the last crop was ready to harvest.

Carmen gazed at the other small gardens, now abandoned for the winter. What fun it had been this summer to swap gardening tips with everyone! Some folks had grown as many as fourteen tomato plants in their little spaces. But the garden right next to Carmen's hadn't produced a thing. Only weeds.

"Why didn't Lucas take care of his garden, Grandpa?" Carmen asked.

"Didn't know how, I guess." Grandpa reached down and yanked a big weed. "A good gardener never gives up. You take care of your plants, and they give you something in return. Your hard work, Carmen, gave you a dozen beautiful pumpkins. They'll each make a fine jack-o-lantern."

It was easy for Carmen to imagine faces on her pumpkins. She had even given her little family names. The one with the yellow patch was called "Goldy." The one with the wrinkled skin she called "Crinkles." The biggest one she called "Grande."

There was even a pumpkin that reminded her of her little sister, so she called it "Lupita."

"I wish I didn't have to give them up," sighed Carmen.

"Now remember, you grew them to sell," said Grandpa. "That's what all the digging and fussing was about."

"I know, I know. I'm just going to miss my big orange babies."

"Well, say 'good night' to your babies. It's suppertime, and I bet you have homework to do."

Carmen blew her pumpkins a kiss. "Sleep tight everybody!"

The next afternoon when Carmen and Grandpa returned, a terrible sight greeted them. The snaky vines were bare, with nothing left but the stems. Someone had kidnapped Carmen's pumpkins!

"Grandpa! Where are they?" gasped Carmen. Her big, brown eyes filled with tears.

"Looks like someone wanted your pumpkins real bad," Grandpa said.

"It's not fair!" Carmen sobbed. "After all our

work!" She stared at the empty vines in disbelief. "Let's go to the farmers' market right now. Maybe we'll find the thief there. And my pumpkins!"

"Now, now," soothed Grandpa. "You can't just go up and accuse someone. You'll have to have proof."

"I'll have proof. Let me get a sack and some things from the garden. Then we'll go."

Soon Carmen and Grandpa were walking the aisles of the huge open-air market. There were tons of pumpkins. Mountains of pumpkins! Carmen was surprised there were so many piles to check out. She stopped and examined each pile slowly before moving on to the next one. Finally, she saw a little group of twelve very familiar-looking pumpkins.

"There they are! Those are my pumpkins!" She pulled Grandpa closer. "See, there's Goldy, and Grande, and Crinkles. And that one is Lupita."

"Young man, are these your pumpkins?" Grandpa asked the boy who was making a FOR SALE sign. When the boy looked up, they saw it was Lucas, the owner of the weedy garden.

"Yeah, they're mine." Lucas went back to work on his sign.

"Oh no, these are my pumpkins!" said Carmen. "You stole them from our garden last night."

"You can't prove that," mumbled Lucas, trying not to meet her angry stare.

Carmen wagged her finger at Lucas. "I'd know my pumpkins anywhere, and these are mine!"

Grandpa patted her shoulder, trying to calm her.

"They sure look like your pumpkins, Carmen, but can you prove it?"

"Yes I can! When something gets broken, you fix it by matching the pieces together, right? Well, in this sack I have the pieces that match my pumpkins."

She opened her sack and dumped it out. Fresh cut stems spilled out over the ground. Carmen sat down and began to match each stem to a pumpkin.

"Look! See how this stem fits this pumpkin? And this one goes to Goldy, and this one fits Crinkles."

Lucas grew restless as Carmen matched stem

after stem. Slowly, he started to back away, ready to run.

One look from Grandpa stopped him cold. "Will you tell us where you got these pumpkins?"

Lucas stared at the ground. "Her garden was always full of things. I couldn't grow anything. Not even a stupid pumpkin."

"You didn't have to steal them," said Carmen. "We would have helped you, right Grandpa?"

"All you had to do was ask, Lucas. In fact, we could become real pests with all our advice."

Lucas ran his hand across the pumpkins. "It looked so easy. Seeds in, pumpkins up. I guess you're pretty angry, huh?"

"I'd feel a lot better if you'd help me sell these pumpkins today," said Carmen. "Then we can start planning for next year."

Lucas looked at her, confused. "Next year?"

"Sure. You don't want to grow weeds again, do you?"

Lucas flashed her a smile and picked up the FOR SALE sign. Before long they had sold every pumpkin but one.

Carmen kept Grande for her jack-o'-lantern. That night she and Lucas scooped out the seeds and divided them. Lucas looked at his pile of seeds and wondered aloud what magic they held. Carmen knew. She could almost imagine the faces of her next big orange babies.

SAUSAGE HEAVEN

Snug inside his mouse hole, Ratón Pepe twitched his whiskery nose. He slowly uncurled his long tail. Why was waking up so hard today? He wiggled his nose again, searching for those yummy breakfast smells. He opened one eye to see if he was still in his own home. Yes, this was the place. Sausage Heaven, the best restaurant in Seville, Spain. But where were the usual smells of fresh coffee, baking bread, and spicy meats?

"Something's wrong," said Pepe, jumping out of bed. "I'd better find Mr. Acosta."

He patted his fur and poked his head out of

his mouse hole. Loud voices drifted down the hall. Pepe scurried off to the kitchen to investigate.

In the kitchen, the rickety smoker-oven stood silent and cold. A jumble of grinders, mixers, and stuffers stuck out in all directions. For a hundred years the smoker-oven had cranked out the best sausages in town.

Pepe hopped over the oily rags and tools on the floor and ducked behind a string of garlic. A big, sooty workman scooted out from behind the oven.

"I'm sorry, Mr. Acosta. This old oven is a wreck. A new one is your only hope," the workman said as he wiped a greasy rag across his face.

"But this oven is one-of-a-kind," said Mr. Acosta. "I can't just go out and buy another one!"

"I might be able to fix it, but it would cost a lot of money." The workman gathered up his tools and went out the door.

Pepe watched a tear roll down Mr. Acosta's cheek. He ran over to him, squeaking words of sympathy. Mr. Acosta's big hands reached down and picked him up.

"Now what will I do, my little friend? I don't have a lot of money. We may soon be out of a home." He gave Pepe a gentle pat.

Pepe jumped down and ran back to his warm bed. He buried his head under the covers. He hoped it was just a bad dream.

But it wasn't a dream. He had to find a way to help his old friend. Unlike most restaurant owners, Mr. Acosta liked having a mouse around. Pepe always cleaned the floor of crumbs, grapes, cheese, or bits of sausages that fell from the tables. Even the customers laughed as Pepe ran from table to table, munching on scraps.

Sometimes he found things he couldn't eat. He dragged them home and shoved them under his straw bed. Pepe hopped down and peered under his bed. "Let's see if I have something that will help," said Pepe. He pulled our six keys, nine hairpins, one comb, five bottle caps, seven buttons, four pens, and two coins. Only two coins. He needed a million coins. But maybe he had the tools to fix the oven.

Out the mouse hole and down the hall, Pepe

dragged his blanket full of treasures. Mr. Acosta still sat like a lump in the kitchen, staring at his broken oven.

Pepe dragged his blanket under the oven and went to work with his "tools." He poked keys into any slot big enough. Why didn't the old oven zoom to life like a race car? He jammed a bottle cap or a button next to any loose or rattling parts. The pens became substitute levers. The comb went under a wobbly leg. Nothing worked.

All he had left were the two coins. Pepe knew that people used them to pay for things. "Bah! Two coins aren't enough," said Pepe. He gave his blanket a shake. The coins rolled across the floor to Mr. Acosta's feet.

"What have you found, Pepe?" asked Mr. Acosta, picking them up. "Ha! One shiny peseta! But what's this?" He looked at the second one for a long time. "I've never seen a coin like this before. Come on, my friend," said Mr. Acosta. "Let's see what we can find out." He picked up Pepe, slipped him into his shirt pocket with the coin, and walked out the door.

When Pepe finally peeked out, he saw they were on a small street lined with busy shops. Mr. Acosta went into a little shop crammed full of books and boxes. Pepe liked this place. It reminded him of his cluttered mouse hole.

"What kind of coin is this?" Mr. Acosta asked the man behind the counter.

The man took out a magnifying glass and studied the coin. Next, he looked in a huge, worn book. He looked at the coin again.

"Where did you find this?" asked the man. "It's more than five hundred years old. It dates back to the time of King Ferdinand and Queen Isabella."

"But is it worth anything?" asked Mr. Acosta.

"In the old days it was worth twenty excelentes."

"I need pesetas, not excelentes. Are you saying this coin is worthless?"

"No sir! According to my book, it's worth about a million pesetas," said the man.

"A million pesetas! For one coin?" Mr. Acosta gasped. "Hooray! We're saved, Pepe!"

A few days later, snug inside his mouse hole, Ratón Pepe woke to delicious smells. His nose twitched, his tail uncurled, and he opened both eyes at once. Mmmm! He smelled fresh coffee, baking bread, and spicy sausages. At last the newly fixed smoker-oven was hard at work cranking out delicious sausages. Pepe would have many more happy years in Sausage Heaven.

TREASURE IN THE DESERT

Luis unlocked the heavy wooden door and pushed it open. Sunlight invaded the dark interior of the old adobe house. The cluttered room looked the same as always, except that Don Sebastian wasn't there to greet him. Luis blinked back his tears. He didn't want to be there.

Luis glanced at the *ristra*, a string of dried chiles hanging by the door. Their musty smell filled the air. How his grandfather had loved those chiles!

He used them in his homemade enchilada sauce and spicy salsas. Luis ran his fingers over the dusty table that took up most of the main room. It was piled with books, papers, and letters. One of the letters caught his eye. It was addressed to him.

As Luis stared at the envelope, his brow wrinkled. Why was there a letter for him? He hardly noticed when his parents lumbered into the house carrying boxes.

"Look at this place!" said his mother. "Don Sebastian never threw anything away. It'll take us days to pack all this up."

His mother always called his grandfather by his formal name. Luis called him *Abuelo.*

"What's that you have, Luis?" asked his father.

"It's a letter for me. I found it on Abuelo's table."

"Well, aren't you going to read it?"

Luis tore open the envelope. "This is weird," he said. "It's from Abuelo. What does this mean?" Luis read aloud:

"A treasure chest I leave to you
It's hidden safe and sound

But you're a clever boy, it's true,

And soon it will be found!"

His mother laughed. "Even though our Don Sebastian has died, he's still up to his old tricks! He loved to play hide-and-seek with our presents. He said it was more fun than just handing them to us."

"Guess he's left you something valuable, Luis," said his father. "But you'll have to find it."

Luis looked around at the piles of Abuelo's things. "It'll take forever! And I don't even know what I'm looking for!"

"Don Sebastian's most valuable possession was his coin collection," said his mother. "He started it as a boy. I bet that's what he left you."

"We have to pack up everything anyway," said his father. "The house will have new owners next week. I hope you find your treasure before then."

Luis started his search in Abuelo's bedroom. First he poked around in the battered chest of drawers. Then he looked under the bed. Nothing but dust balls there. He tugged the mattress to the floor. No luck. He felt behind all the books on the bookshelves. This was harder than he'd thought.

His mother and father filled box after box with Abuelo's things. Clothes and kitchen items would go to the mission house. Furniture and sentimental items would come home with them. Everything was checked carefully.

By evening they had cleared away most of the clutter. A big pile of trash waited by the front door, spoiling the beauty of the nearby cactus. They sat around Don Sebastian's old wooden table eating take-out chicken for dinner.

Luis reread his mysterious letter a dozen times, looking for a clue. *A treasure chest. . .* Could that mean a big box? *Hidden safe and sound. . .* Did Abuelo have a safe? Luis scanned the smooth adobe walls. Nothing looked like a place for a safe. He looked at the envelope. The stamps were very pretty.

"Are these stamps valuable?" Luis asked.

His father studied them under the light. "Nope. They're nice, but not old enough. Don Sebastian also put way too much postage on that letter."

Luis looked at the stamps again. One thirteen-cent stamp had a picture of an adobe house, like the one they were in. Next came a twenty-cent stamp with a saguaro cactus on it. After that was a diamond-shaped stamp, worth ten cents, showing a picture of petrified wood. The last stamp read "Banking and Commerce." It was worth ten cents, too. Fifty-three cents for a one-page letter. It wasn't like Abuelo to waste money.

Money! Luis stared at the last stamp, the "Banking and Commerce" one. The design was all coins. He banged the table with his fist. I know where the treasure is! These stamps are telling the story. See, this is like Abuelo's adobe house," said Luis, pointing to the first stamp. "This saguaro cactus must be the one near the door."

Luis ran outside. Sure enough, a tall saguaro loomed dark against the sunset. He looked down at the base of the cactus. He knew what he would find. A huge chunk of petrified wood sat nestled in the dirt. He tugged at the heavy stone until he had pushed it aside.

His mother brought out a small shovel, and it

48

wasn't long before Luis and his mom unearthed a heavy metal chest. Inside, hundreds of shiny coins—silver dollars, Indian-head pennies, and others—winked up at him.

Not far away, a covey of quail chittered as they ducked for cover under some bushes. Luis smiled. "It sounds like Abuelo is laughing at me out there."

"Yes," agreed his mother. "If he were here, he'd be having a good chuckle over how he made you search. You must have inherited his brains as well as his coins. He knew that you would figure out the message!"

THE TROLL WEDDING

Way up north in the mountains of Norway, a young lass named Karla sat fishing from a rock in the middle of the river. Karla didn't notice the tiny red eyes that watched her from the forest. She didn't notice when a hairy troll climbed up the rock behind her.

"Who you?" asked the troll.

Karla almost jumped into the water, she was so surprised.

"Who are you?" she asked.

"Uff-da," replied the troll. "You're not from around here, I can tell. You don't have a tail."

Sure enough, Karla noticed that Uff-da had something that looked like a cow's tail wagging and dragging behind him.

"You're not human, I can tell. What are you?"

"I'm a troll, of course. And you're sitting on our special rock."

"What makes it so special?"

"All of our important events happen on this rock. Today my daughter Ugla is getting married right here."

"On a rock?"

"Of course. We make a wedding bridge first. You come to the party, ja?" Uff-da grabbed Karla's arm and whisked her across the water and into the forest.

"I must be dreaming all this," mumbled Karla to herself. But she didn't want to make the troll angry. An angry troll might use his magic to turn her into something slimy, like a frog.

Uff-da led Karla deeper into the dark forest. The pine trees were so thick that only a little sun filtered through their branches. "Too much sun for a wedding!" said the troll. He hopped on his left foot and muttered something in troll-speak. Suddenly the forest got darker. A cold wind blew through the trees, and snow fell everywhere.

Karla's teeth chattered. "You want it cold and snowy?" she asked, pulling her sweater tighter.

"Best for a wedding. Everything is white!"

Next, Uff-da took Karla to the cave where Ugla was getting ready for her big day. They watched as several lady trolls fussed over the bride. One lady troll combed Ugla's snarly hair into a lovely green blob. "However did you decide to marry Alfi?" she asked Ugla.

"Oh, there were several fellows who crawled out from their rocks to court me. But I was very picky," Ugla said. "I made them all go through many difficult tests."

"What kind of tests?" another friend asked, handing Ugla a broken mirror.

"First, I made a big pot of moldy mushroom stew. And the messiest eater was my Alfi!"

"Wonderful! What was the next test?" another troll lady asked.

"The mushroom stew made those boys very

tired. So they stretched out on the ground and soon were fast asleep, snoring like pigs. And my Alfi was the loudest!"

"You lucky girl! Then what?"

"While they were all asleep, I sniffed the toes of each fellow. And my Alfi's were the stinkiest!" said Ugla.

"Oh, what a clever troll you are!" her friend cried.

It seemed to Karla that trolls had very different ideas of what was proper. But she kept quiet. Maybe if she was polite they'd let her go home.

Uff-da then took her to another part of the forest where cook trolls were busy making the wedding cake. They mixed in two dozen rotten eggs; a gallon of sour milk; and twenty scoops of crunchy flour, full of bugs. When it was all done, they whipped up a frosting of dark green pond scum.

"Isn't that lovely?" said Uff-da.

Karla nodded and gulped, hoping she wouldn't have to eat any of it. Just then, a sound like mooing cows filled the air.

"Ah, the wedding chimes!" said Uff-da. "Time to begin."

Trolls jumped out from every tree and rock and scrambled to a clearing. The cook trolls pushed the wedding cake to the center. On the count of ONE! everybody grabbed a handful of cake and shoved it into their mouths. Next, they filled their mugs with fishy river water.

"Skoal, to Ugla and Alfi!" they shouted.

At last it was time for the ceremony. The trolls wiped their mouths on their sleeves and pushed their way into line.

"Hear Ye! Make way for the bride and groom!" someone shouted.

Ugla glowed like a firefly, waddling beside the groom. Alfi grinned a toothless smile and nodded to all he saw. Behind them came Uff-da, plunking out a polka on his tail. The Official Joiner was next in line, and the rest of the trolls followed.

When they reached the river's edge, Karla noticed that a delicate bridge of twigs had been built over to the special rock.

The Joiner led the trolls onto the twiggy bridge.

It swayed back and forth over the rushing water of the river. Karla stayed behind. She didn't want to risk adding her weight to the bridge.

"Like a bridge joins two sides, let us join these two," the Joiner said solemnly. Then he chanted the wedding words to Ugla and Alfi. "Mo ho du leva! Hundra, hundra or!" And with that, he tied their tails together.

"Hoo-hah! Hoo-hah!" shouted the trolls. They clapped their furry hands and stomped their gnarly feet. Someone pushed Karla into the crowd to meet the happy couple. It was too much for the little bridge. The twigs snapped, dumping everyone into the freezing river.

"What a fun wedding!" the trolls yelled as they bounced out of the icy water and scampered into the trees.

Shivering, Karla crawled back up onto the rock. Uff-da was standing on the river's edge, waving his arms at the sky. The sun came out and the snow disappeared.

"I told you it was a special rock," said Uff-da.

"Did all this really happen?" asked Karla.

"Would I pull your tail?" said the troll.

"But I don't have a tail."

"Exactly!" And quick as a blink, the little troll tumbled like a ball into the dark forest.

BLIND AMBITION

The Monday morning crush of students bustled to class at Spruce Middle School. Jenny Snyder paused in the hallway, checking if she'd remembered to put her homework in her bag. She felt a tap on her shoulder, turned and almost bumped into her best friend, Kris Olson.

"Hey, how was your weekend?"

Jenny shrugged. "The usual. What about you?"

"It was great," said Kris, shifting her backpack. "We spent the whole time skiing. You should have seen my crazy brother fly over the moguls."

"No broken legs?"

"Not yet!" said Kris.

Jenny smiled. It was always the same with Kris and her family. They found so many ways to go off and have fun. Jenny wished her own life wasn't so quiet. She longed to do something daring—something she could brag about some Monday morning at school.

"Sounds like fun," said Jenny with a sigh. "Since we moved to Colorado, all anyone talks about is going skiing. Wish I could go."

"But you could!" said Kris, grasping Jenny's arm.

"Are you serious? Haven't you forgotten something?" asked Jenny.

"What, that you're blind?"

"Duh! You know I'd smash into the very first tree."

"Not a chance. Up at Crystal Park, where we ski, there are programs designed for skiers with disabilities, including blind skiers. They've been doing it for years."

"Really? Wow!" Thoughts of going fast, of swishing down a snow packed slope, filled Jenny's head. She felt a prickle of excitement run up her neck. Could this finally be her chance to be a daredevil?

"Why don't you come up with us next weekend?" urged Kris. "I'll introduce you to one of the instructors. You'll have a blast."

"I. . .I don't know if I could do it," said Jenny.

"Sure you could. You'll be with pros who know how to teach you."

Jenny hesitated. A smile tugged at her cheeks. "I'll have to ask my parents."

The next Saturday, Jenny stepped out of the van at Crystal Park. Kris and her family clattered around her, unloading all their gear.

Jenny inhaled the icy air laced with the smell of piñon smoke from the lodge. Here she was, ready or not. As she waited for Kris's family to unload their skis she wondered, *Could I really do this?* Kris's words echoed in her mind: *Sure you could!*

"Good luck, Jen!" called Mrs. Olson. "I made arrangements for you with an instructor. She's waiting for you now."

Kris and Jenny crunched their way over the snowy path to the ski school office. A cheery voice welcomed them inside.

"This is my friend Jenny," said Kris. "She has one ambition in life—to ski like the wind!"

A firm hand grasped Jenny's. "You've come to the right place, then. My name is Britt. I'll be your instructor."

"And guardian angel, I hope," said Jenny with a nervous laugh.

Kris gave her a squeeze on the arm. "I'll check with you later. Have fun!"

Jenny knew Kris was eager to join her family on the slopes. Now it was up to her and Britt to make this adventure work. Today she would find out if she had the nerve to be a daredevil.

After Jenny was fitted with boots, skis and poles, Britt slipped a silky vest over her head.

"This tells others on the slope that you're a skier who's blind. I wear one that says 'Instructor of the Blind.' Everyone gives us the right of way, so don't worry about people bumping into us."

It felt strange sliding along on skis. In regular

shoes, Jenny could feel the ground under her feet. But with heavy boots and skis, it all felt so different. It was almost like floating.

She and Britt spent most of the morning on the flat areas and the "Bunny Slope," getting Jenny used to managing the skis. She learned how to stand, walk, slide, snowplow, and most important, how to stop. There was even a lesson on falling down in a gentle way so she wouldn't get hurt.

Britt had a warm and patient voice. She talked Jenny through every move. She had that same "you can do it" attitude that Kris had. Jenny guessed she must be older—seventeen, maybe. After a little practice, Jenny was ready to try her first real ski slope.

As they waited for the chair lift, Jenny's nerves fluttered like butterflies in her stomach. She took a deep breath. Was she excited or just scared? She'd have to trust Britt with her every move and listen to her instructions.

"We're next," said Britt, guiding her into place. "Get ready to sit. One, two—now!"

Jenny felt the chair bump behind her legs and she plopped back confidently.

"Super! You act like you've done this all your life," said Britt.

"I wish!" Jenny liked the sensation of riding the lift, swaying gently as they climbed. The spicy smell of pines told her they were passing over a forested area. When they neared the top, Britt gave her the "stand up" cue, then guided her toward the beginner slope.

"Remember, Jenny, when I say turn left, point your knees and ankles left. Point them right for right turns. Keep your weight forward, knees bent."

Jenny pushed off and began to glide down the slope with Britt right beside her.

"You're doing fine!" Britt assured her.

But then, somehow, the tips of her skis crossed and Jenny tumbled forward, sliding several feet in a belly flop along the snow. Her skis snapped free of her boots and her legs went sprawling. Hot tears stung her eyes.

"You OK?" Britt asked, crouching near her.

"Yeah," Jenny sniffed. She wiped a tear away with her gloved hand. "But it's so embarrassing! I must look like a total fool!"

"Don't worry about it, Jen. Everyone here on the slope has done exactly what you just did, at least once, probably more. It's no big deal. You just get up and keep going."

Britt helped her get her skis on again and stand up, ready for a new run. Another skier breezed by them and shouted, "Been there, done that!"

Jenny laughed. "Now I feel foolish for crying. Let's get back to the lesson."

Britt kept up a constant chatter down the hill. She told Jenny when to turn, when to slow down, and what the conditions were like.

"We're coming to a nice, gentle run now. Let's go a little faster," said Britt.

The cold air whooshed across Jenny's face. "Wow! I'm sailing through the wind! This is so awesome!"

It was a first for her. She'd heard her friends speed by on their bikes or skateboards and she'd always wondered what it must feel like to have the wind rush by you. Now she knew. It felt great.

Jenny and Britt skied the beginner slope three more times that day, stopping only for lunch. With each pass, Jenny grew more confident, in spite of a few more tumbles in the snow. For the first time in her life, she felt free—free to do things other kids did, free to dare, free to feel the wind.

WHISPERS IN THE NIGHT

"Sleep tight. Don't let the bedbugs bite."

"Same to you, Mom."

Casey bent down and checked the floor. It wasn't bedbugs he worried about. It was scorpions and snakes. He hated living in the desert! But the doctor had said that Mom needed a drier climate. So as soon as school was out, they'd moved from humid Kentucky to the Arizona desert.

It was dry all right. Instead of soft grass, clumps of spiky cactus surrounded the houses in the neighborhood. Even the wall around their yard had something growing there that looked like dried snakes.

But the nighttime was the worst. Then the desert came alive with strange sounds that sent chills up Casey's spine. What were those screeching, yipping, and snorting things out there? He had heard about coyotes, Gila monsters, and some piggy critter called a javelina. But he hadn't seen any—yet.

Casey pulled the thin sheet up and tried to think brave thoughts. *I'm twelve years old!* he reminded himself. *I can't be the family scaredy cat. Mom needs me.*

Finally, sleep shut down all his thoughts.

After a couple of hours, something woke Casey. He propped himself up and listened. Whispers drifted in the open window. Slowly, he knelt at the window above his bed and peeked under the shade. Shadowy figures moved along the wall, flicking flashlights as they went. Were there burglars out there? He held his breath and listened harder.

"This is the place," the first voice said.

"Yeah," answered a second person.

"But is the time right?"

"We'll soon find out!"

Casey didn't wait to hear more. He leaped out of bed and flicked on the light. Maybe if he let them know he'd seen them, they'd go away. Then he ran into the kitchen and turned that light on, too. He listened for more sounds by the front door. Silence. Nothing. Good! They were gone.

He crawled back into bed, determined to stay alert. But the next thing he knew, it was morning. Gentle doves cooed on the windowsill. Bright sunlight sparkled outside. Last night's noises and spooky shadows had faded like a dream.

He found his mom having breakfast on the patio.

"Sleep OK, Mom?" Casey asked.

"Like a baby," she answered. "I think this desert air has already helped me."

"That's good." Casey decided not to mention that he thought burglars had been casing the house. No need to worry her. Whoever it was, they probably wouldn't be back.

But he was wrong. The next night Casey heard voices again.

"Look!" someone whispered. "You were right!"

"A real treasure!" another person said.

Casey peeked outside. He saw two heads bobbing along the wall. He didn't wake his mom. She needed her rest. He'd have to risk going outside alone. He pushed away thoughts of snakes and scorpions. Grabbing his flashlight, he slipped out the back door.

Moonlight cast eerie shadows across the yard. He edged around the cactus until he was even with the wall. The strangers whispered on the opposite side.

"How lovely!" a woman's voice said.

"This was well worth the wait," a man replied.

Lovely? What were they talking about?

Casey popped his head around the corner of the wall. A man and a woman stood by the snaky vines. The lady spotted him and waved him over.

"Come look! The cereus are blooming!"

"Huh?" Casey eased out of the shadows and came closer.

The things that were so ugly and snaky by day had produced a dozen star-like flowers.

"We've been checking for a week now," said the man.

"This is night-blooming cereus. It blooms only one night a year," added the woman.

Casey blinked. "So you're the people I heard last night," he murmured.

The woman looked apologetic. "We're Mr. and Mrs. Miller. We live down the street. I'm sorry if we woke you. We tried to be quiet."

Casey sighed with relief. "That's OK," he told his neighbors. "I'm glad you woke me." He gazed again at the plant that was filled with white flowers. "No wonder you kept coming back. The cereus is really beautiful."

When Casey headed back into the house a few minutes later, he glanced up at the sky. Millions of bright stars glittered above. Off in the distance a coyote yipped "hello" to the moon. Maybe the desert isn't so scary after all, he thought.

LUCIA FOR GRANDMA

Karin's grandmother was leaving her. She was going back home to Sweden. But there were no suitcases to pack. And there was no ticket to buy. Grandma's trip was only in her mind.

It started one day when Grandma picked up her purse, walked out the door saying, "*Gå hem nu.*" Go home now.

"But you are home, Grandma," said Karin, patting her arm and leading her back into the house.

"*Ja, hem nu.*" She sat back down in her cozy chair.

Karin understood only a few words in Swedish. When her grandmother had come to America, she had worked hard to learn English. There was no time for teaching others the old language. Karin desperately wished she had learned more words. She loved her grandmother. But now, as she saw Grandma enter into the world of the past, Karin wondered how she would talk with her. How would she tell her she loved her?

On her good days, Grandma knew who Karin was and talked with her a little in English. "Come, tell me about your day," she would say. Those were the best times. Karin snuggled close to her on the sofa and shared all her adventures.

But in early December, Grandma stopped speaking English completely. Instead, she began singing in Swedish. Over and over she sang about someone named Lucia.

"Who is this 'Lucia' Grandma sings about?" Karin asked her mom.

"That must be Santa Lucia," her mom explained. "Long ago, there was a young girl in Italy who helped the poor. She brought food to people living in dark caverns. To light her way, she wore candles on her head."

"Candles on her head! Didn't her hair catch fire?"

"No. She was very careful. Anyway, Sweden adopted Lucia Day from Italy. You see, wintertime in Sweden is dark and gloomy. Lucia reminds people that soon they will have more light and longer days. So early on December 13, the oldest daughter becomes Lucia. She wears a crown of candles and a white dress with a red sash. She brings saffron rolls and coffee to the family."

"Were you ever Lucia, Mom?"

"No. We didn't keep up the tradition. But I think we have a CD here of Swedish Christmas music, including the Lucia song."

Karin's mother found the CD in a packing box full of Christmas odds and ends. On the front of the plastic cover was a picture of Lucia—white dress, red sash, and a crown of candles on her head. She looked like an angel.

Day after day, Karin watched her grandmother wander around the house humming her song. Karin missed their talks together. She wished she could wear a white dress, have candles in her hair, and be Lucia for Grandma. But her fantasy soon evaporated. Her mother would never let her put candles on her head.

"But maybe there is a way," said Karin to herself. She ran to her room and rummaged through the closet. There she found an old white flannel nightgown. "This will do just fine! Now for one more thing. . . ." Tucked in her dresser, under sweaters and socks, was just what she needed—a bright red scarf that could be her sash. But what about the candles? She didn't want to set her hair on fire or get it full of wax drippings.

That night at dinner, Karin listened as Grandma babbled on and on in Swedish. Her mother nodded and said, "*Ja, ja.*" Karin didn't think her mother really understood. It was a game they played, and it made Grandma happy. Karin carefully watched four candles flicker on the table. It was already December 12th. How was she going to be Lucia without candles? Then she smiled. She had the answer.

Before going to bed, Karin laid out all the things she would need in the morning. She set her alarm for six o'clock and tucked it under her pillow.

Karin woke up with a start when the alarm sounded its muffled buzz. Quickly, she shut it off before anyone else heard it. She changed into her white nightgown, tied the red scarf around her waist, and tiptoed downstairs. While the coffee was brewing, she popped the CD into the player. Then she quietly carried the player and the four candles from the table into Grandma's room. The tall dresser was just the right height for the candles. She hurried back to the kitchen to collect the tray of cookies and coffee.

When Karin got back to Grandma's room, she reached up and lit the candles on the dresser. Then she stood beneath them with her tray. She was sure it would look as if the candles ere on her head. She took a deep breath and pushed the Start button on the CD player. Heavenly music filled the air:

Sankta Lu-cia . . . .

Sankta Lu-cia. . . .

Grandma woke, lifted her head and stared at Karin.

"*Är du en angel?*" she asked.

"She wants to know if you're an angel, Karin." Her mother stood in the doorway, beaming at her.

"No, Grandma. I'm Santa Lucia."

"*Ja, ja. Lucia.*" Every line in Grandma's face melted into a smile. Then she sighed happily. "*Hem nu!*"

"Yes, you're home now," said Karin's mother.

The joy on Grandma's face that morning made Karin feel warm all over. For just a little while, all of them were *hem nu*. Home now, in Sweden.

Karin had found a way to tell Grandma she loved her.

PADDY O'POOLE

One fine March day, a leprechaun named Paddy O'Poole saw a shaggy brown dog trotting down the road.

"Ah, that's what I need," said Paddy, "a pet to liven me lonely life."

When the dog scampered away, the leprechaun jumped up and followed her.

The dog trotted to her house and slipped in through a doggy door. Paddy edged up to a window and peeked inside. T'was a fine place, indeed, and by gosh it was all decorated for a St. Patrick's Day party. Green balloons bobbed from chair backs and doorknobs. A rainbow of streamers stretched across the living room. In the middle of the floor sat a fair young lass gluing paper shamrocks to a most unusual box.

On top of the box there was hole and a sign which read, "Free Gold." Now those were words to gladden Paddy's heart. For next to shamrocks and rainbows, gold was his most favorite thing.

"Your box looks beautiful, Kelly," said her mother, Mrs. Ward. "Now, let's go pick up the cake for our party."

Kelly turned to her dog and held his fuzzy chin in her hand. "If you see a leprechaun, Ginger, you chase him into my trap, okay?"

Ginger wagged her tail, then licked Kelly's hand.

As soon as Kelly and her mother were gone, Paddy stuck his head through the doggy door. A wet tongue covered his face in kisses. "Get back, fuzz face," shouted Paddy. "Let me in so I can see this fine trap your lass has made for me."

The little dog ran over to the box and sniffed in the hole. Paddy sniffed, too. "How very strange," he said, scratching his wild red beard. "Gold isn't supposed to smell sweet."

Paddy reached inside and drew out three round pieces wrapped in gold foil. "Ah, 'tis only chocolate," he said. He unwrapped the candy coins and popped them into his mouth.

"Rworf!" barked Ginger.

"Oh, no. Chocolate isn't good for you," said Paddy. "But if ye come home with me, I'll give ye grand treats, for sure." Paddy reached out to grab Ginger. But she leaped away and darted into another room. The leprechaun scratched his beard again. This was harder than he thought. Maybe he could use the box to catch her. In the kitchen he found some dog biscuits and dropped them into the hole.

"Come here to me now, ye fine ball of fur," he called. The dog scampered over to the box. This time, when she stuck her nose in the hole, Paddy gave her head an extra pat and, PUM! Ginger was stuck.

"Now I've got me a pet!" cried Paddy, tying on a pink streamer leash. But at the doggy door he stopped. Ginger would never fit through now. The box had to come off. But no matter how hard he pulled, it wouldn't budge. Then Paddy spied the green balloons. They might help lift the box, he thought. He grabbed a bunch and tied them onto the box. But one balloon escaped and sailed up to the ceiling where it hit the ceiling fan and went,

POP!

The noise sent Ginger tearing through the house, box on her head, knocking over chairs and setting off the burglar alarm.

BRRRRrrrrring!

Alarm bells clanged and whooped.

Ginger barked and yelped as she ran from room to room.

Paddy closed his eyes and clapped his hands over his ears. "Oh no," he moaned.

Outside, a siren wailed like a banshee, coming closer and closer until a police car screeched to a stop in the driveway. Paddy climbed up on a bookcase and peered through the window. Red and blue lights flashed. Two policemen jumped out of the car and strode toward the house.

"Come out with your hands up!" called one officer."Rworf!" barked Ginger. She raced through the house again, crashing into more lamps and tables. Three green balloons exploded.

POP!

POP!   POP!

Just when Paddy thought things couldn't get any worse, another car pulled into the driveway. Kelly and her mother had arrived home.

"What's going on?" asked Mrs. Ward.

"There's a burglar in your house," replied the officer.

"Or a monster!" added his partner, pointing to a strange figure in the window. "But we've got him covered—I think."

"Rworf!"

"That's no monster," cried Kelly. "That's Ginger!"

She and her mother ran to open the door.

Kelly pulled the box from Ginger's head and laughed. "You silly dog! How did you get caught in my leprechaun trap?" Ginger gave her a sloppy kiss, then ran straight for Paddy's hiding place under the table.

"Shoo! Get away," Paddy whispered, waving

his hands. "I'll be in fierce trouble if they catch me."

But it was too late. There stood Kelly staring right at him, her eyes wide. "Ginger, you *did* catch a leprechaun!"

Paddy sighed and shrugged his arms in surrender. "Aye, lass, 'tis true. Now go and fetch your mother so I can grant you yer three wishes."

"Guard him, Ginger!" said Kelly as she ran to get her mother.

But in the blink of a fairy's eye, Paddy zipped out to the patio, past the pool, and escaped. For that's what happens if you slip up and take your eyes off a leprechaun, even for a moment.

Back in the park, Paddy O'Poole sat on a rock and tried to calm his pounding heart. Perhaps his life would be better without a dog. He didn't need so much excitement. Just then, a silvery unicorn trotted by. Each time his hoof struck the earth, a golden nugget popped out. Paddy rubbed his eyes in wonder.

"'Tis the luck o' the Irish, to be sure," he said, chasing after the unicorn. "There goes the perfect pet for me!"

GULLYWASHER GULCH

Ebenezer Overall lived in a rickety shack above
the town of Dry Gulch. His shack was so full of
stuff it looked ready to slide down the hill. When
folks stopped by to visit they'd just stand in the
doorway and gawk.

"You should get rid of this stuff," they said,
pointing to the barrels of nails, tools, beans and
crockery. But old Eb shook his head. "Nope. I'm
savin' up for a rainy day. You never know when
it'll come in handy."

Eb's yard was just as crowded. In between piles of lumber, stacks of shingles, and bundles of tarpaper, Eb grew five kinds of beans in a little garden. Come fall he'd harvest them, dry them out, and pour them into another barrel.

When his sister Ella May came to visit she'd say, "Ebenezer Overall, you're just an old pack rat. Why in tarnation do you need all this stuff?"

"I'm savin' it for a rainy day," Eb would answer. "You never know what'll happen."

When Eb wasn't growing beans or saving nails, he did a little prospecting. For nearly fifty years he'd hiked the rugged mountains behind his shack, looking for gold. The townsfolk figured he'd found some, too—a strike worth millions.

"Wish he'd tell us where the gold is," Mayor Dan grumbled. "We could all use a few nuggets."

But old Eb kept quiet. Whenever he came back from the mountains with shiny gold nuggets in his pocket, he'd wait until dark and dig a little hole. Then he'd reach down, drop in a pouch full of gold, and pat the sand over the hole.

"You stay put now. Some rainy day I'll be

needin' ya." But since rain was as scarce as a jackalope, he figured that'd be a while.

That summer it was so dry the sun came up as a big ball of dust.

It was so hot that the lizards hobbled around on stick crutches so they wouldn't burn their scaly toes.

Why, it was so hot that when Eb made his breakfast he just set his coffeepot in the sun and waited for it to boil. The coffee went down real good with his rock-fried eggs and sand-warmed beans.

One sizzly morning Eb decided to go prospecting. He packed up his burro and headed for the hills. He noticed the air had a mighty peculiar scent to it—real spicy-like. But he paid it no mind and set about digging up more nuggets.

About midday a rumble in the sky made him look up. Dark clouds billowed overhead. Lighting flashed and then...KER-RACK!

"Well, it's about time!" cried Eb. He grabbed his shovel and burro and hightailed it back to his shack while fat raindrops splattered in the dust.

"Hope it's not one of those skittery storms," he muttered to his burro. "The kind that spits a few drops and then disappears."

But this cloud looked like it might want to sit a spell, and so it did. The rain came down like someone had unzipped a heavenly ocean. The thirsty ground and plants slurped up every drop.

Eb sat in his shack, watching and worrying. He knew the desert couldn't handle too much rain all at once. He kept his eye on the nearby gully. It was normally a dry wash, but now it churned with gushy brown water. Soon a tumbling torrent came roaring straight toward Eb's shack.

First, the old shack trembled. Then it shook. Then it splintered. SWOOSH! That gullywasher carried Eb and all his stuff right down the hillside toward town. Clinging to his burro, he rode those rapids like a rodeo cowboy.

By the time the rain stopped, the town was a shambles. Every building had washed away. Folks had grabbed on to any old post, hanging on for dear life. Now they looked a lot like mud-covered stick lizards on a hot summer day.

"We're ruined!" sighed Mayor Dan.

"What'll we do?" cried Sheriff Amos.

"What's this?" asked little Miranda, opening her fist. "I found it in the mud. Is it gold?"

The mere whisper of gold set everyone to work, cleaning and scraping off mud. When they were done, they'd found gold nuggets all over. The big round lumps in the middle of the street turned out to be barrels of nails, tools, beans and crockery. The square lumps were bundles of wood, tarpaper and shingles.

"But it all belongs to Eb," said little Miranda. "Can we use it?"

A hush fell over the crowd. Every face turned toward Ebenezer Overall.

"Sure as shootin'!" said Eb. "We'll build us a new town and we'll call it Gullywasher Gulch."

"We're saved!" said Mayor Dan.

"It's a miracle!" said Preacher Stan.

"It's what I've been tellin' ya," said Eb. "I was savin' it all for a rainy gullywasher day just like this."

PUMA PAYS A VISIT

One summer morning Coyote saw Puma coming down from the mountains.

"What brings you to the desert?" asked Coyote.

"I'm lookin' for adventure," said Puma.

"Well, Fox has invited me for lunch," said Coyote. "Want to come?"

"Why not?" said Puma. "I'm sure she'll be delighted to meet me."

So Puma and Coyote trotted off through the desert.

"What funny-looking trees," said Puma, pointing to a tall cactus. "They don't have any leaves."

"Those aren't trees!" explained Coyote. "They're saguaros. They have stickers instead of leaves. They can live for two hundred years and grow over sixty feet tall."

"Big deal!" huffed Puma, stretching his arms up high. "Why, where I come from the trees grow so tall they reach the sky and scratch the rain out of the clouds."

"Oh, really?" said Coyote, flicking his tail.

Coyote led Puma down into a dry wash where Javelina was munching on some cactus pads.

"We get rain in the desert, don't we, Javelina?" asked Coyote.

Javelina snorted. "Are you kidding? Remember that rain storm last year? I had to hoof it outta this river real fast."

Puma snickered. "You call this a river? Why, where I come from the rivers are so full of water, we use giant trout to haul the boats across from one side to the other."

"You don't say!" said Coyote, not believing a word of it.

As they climbed out of the wash, something sped toward them in a whirlwind of dust.

"Who's that?" asked Puma.

"It's Jackrabbit," replied Coyote. "Hey, Jackrabbit! Stop a minute!"

Jackrabbit jogged in circles around them. "Can't stop. Can't stop," he gasped. "I'm getting ready for another race. Bye-bye!" And he took off running again.

"Is that all he does? Run races?" exclaimed Puma. "Why, where I come from the rabbits grow as big as cows. They give milk in the morning and churn it into butter by night."

"What, they don't lay eggs, too?" mocked Coyote.

Before Puma could answer, a shadow crossed over the ground. Puma looked up at the sky and asked, "What's that tiny thing up there?"

Coyote clenched his teeth. "That's no tiny thing. "That's Hawk. He's looking for a tender mouse for his lunch."

"A hawk?" sneered Puma. "Why, were I come from the hawks have such big wings, they carry herds of buffalo from one field to another all summer long."

Coyote covered his eyes with his paws. What a tale-teller!

"Speaking of lunch," said Puma. "When do we eat? I'm starving."

Coyote sighed. Maybe inviting Puma along wasn't such a good idea.

Over the next hill they found Fox spreading out the picnic under a broad mesquite tree.

"Thanks for coming, Coyote," said Fox. "It's good you brought a friend. There's a pile of food here. Please, help yourself."

So Puma did. He gobbled up all the cactus pad salad. He swallowed all the jalapeño corn bread. He slurped up all the quail eggs.

"Something to drink?" asked Fox, trying to ignore that Puma hadn't left a crumb for her or Coyote.

In one long gulp, Puma downed the whole jar of prickly pear juice. He didn't leave a single drop.

"Interesting snacks," said Puma. "But where I come from. . ."

Coyote interrupted. "I know. The food is much tastier. Much fancier. MUCH BIGGER!"

"Riiiight," said Puma, yawning. "Time for my nap now." He stretched out in the shade and soon was fast asleep.

"That does it!" sputtered Coyote. "That braggart

makes me sick. He's worse than I am!"

Fox's eyes grew wide. "That's hard to believe."

"Believe it!" said Coyote. "But, I know how to shut him up!"

Coyote trotted off to find Tortoise and his family. When he found them, he explained his plan.

"Well, if it doesn't take too long," drawled Tortoise. "I have another race with Jackrabbit today. He lost the last one, you know."

"Don't worry," assured Coyote. "If my plan works, you'll be done in a few minutes."

Coyote brought Tortoise and his family over where Puma was sleeping. Very carefully, Coyote and Fox placed them on Puma's big tummy.

Puma twitched.

Then he sighed.

Then he opened his eyes and screamed.

"AAAAHHH! GET THESE MONSTERS OFF ME!"

"Don't be afraid, dear Puma," purred Fox. "Can't you see? Those aren't monsters."

"Noooo," added Coyote. "They're just desert

fleas. And they're the tiny ones, too. Most of our fleas are MUCH bigger. Where we come from..."

But Puma didn't wait to hear the rest. He was already running back to the mountains.

"Look at him," said Coyote. "He said he wanted adventure."

"And that's exactly what he got!" said Fox.

THE MESSAGE OF THE COQUI

Antonio and his grandmother sat at the table sharing a breakfast of *café con leche* and buttered toast. Dozens of boxes and bundles surrounded them, the result of three days of packing. After living most of her life on an old farm raising goats, Nana had decided to move into a small apartment in the Puerto Rican capital of San Juan.

"We make a good team," Antonio said. "But I still wish you would come and live with us in New York. It's really exciting there."

Nana laughed. "I have plenty of excitement here, too. Besides, how could I leave my beautiful island with its tropical flowers and birds?"

Antonio had to agree that Puerto Rico was beautiful. His grandmother lived in a dense rain forest called El Yunque. The same scraggly plants Antonio's mother grew in little pots back home grew into giants that reached for the sky here. In some places the growth was so thick, it nearly blotted out the sun. His whole family used to live here, but had moved to New York just after he was born fourteen years ago.

"I'm glad Mom let me come to help you move," said Antonio. "One of the things I like here is listening to the birds that sing at night."

Nana chuckled. "Those aren't birds, Antonio. You're hearing the coquís."

"Yeah, that's just how they sound. Ko-KEE! Ko-KEE! What are they?"

"'The coquí is a small frog," Nana explained.

"They're all over the island. They sing out all night unless they sense danger. Then they're quiet. They like to tell us that all is well."

Nana glanced out the window, her face serious. "The little frogs got quiet last night because a storm is moving in."

Antonio followed her gaze. Sure enough, the sky was growing darker. The wind pushed through the palm trees, making them bend and sway.

"You'd better go down to the fields and bring back the goats. They could get lost in bad weather," Nana said, her hand gripping his arm. "Hurry! These island storms can come fast."

Antonio was out the door in a flash, running along the path that led to the fields. Dark mountains loomed over him on one side and leafy trees reached out to him on the other. The busy city life of New York seemed like another planet compared to this awesome jungle. As he ran, he spotted a cave on a hillside.

It would only take a minute to check out, thought Antonio. Twisted vines hung like snakes across the entrance. Inside, it was dark and damp. It wasn't very deep but was big enough to stand up in. It would make a cool hideout for three or four people. The howl of the wind outside reminded him of his errand. The storm had gotten a lot worse in just a few minutes. Nana was right. He had to hurry.

Antonio found the goats huddled together, bleating in fear. They didn't like the wind any more than he did. Stinging drops of rain began hitting his face. Quickly moving the goats along, he pushed them into the wind. A strange darkness covered the sky. He wondered if they would make it back to Nana's house in time. Out of the corner of his eye he saw something huge fly toward him. He hit the ground as a piece of roof sailed over his head like a giant piece of tissue paper.

Nana! Maybe that was part of her roof that almost hit him. She couldn't stay for long in her creaky old house. Maybe the cave would be a better place.

The goats trotted ahead of him, sensing the danger. They made it back to Nana's house which was shaking wildly.

"I'm so glad you're back!" Nana was crying and hugging him at the same time.

"Come on, Nana, we can't stay here. I know a better place."

He made Nana walk between two of the goats, holding on to clumps of hair on their necks. They gave her steady support and kept her from falling on the way to the old cave.

The storm raged for hours. While they waited, Nana told stories about other storms she'd experienced on the island. When the winds died down and the rain stopped, they climbed slowly back up the muddy path.

Nana sighed in relief when she saw her house. "It's still standing!"

That evening, after they had cleaned up the debris in the yard, Antonio asked, "Why do you want to stay in Puerto Rico when you can have such terrible storms?"

Nana smiled at him. "My island is full of beauty, including powerful storms. That's part of our excitement here. But tonight will be calm and quiet."

"How do you know that?" asked Antonio.

"Because a little 'bird' tells me so!" She winked and tilted her head to listen.

Antonio listened, too, and smiled. He heard the simple two-word song coming from the bushes. "Ko-KEE! Ko-KEE!" Once again the little frogs were announcing that all was well.

ALONE UNDER THE STARS

Patty gave her dog, Boomer, a pat as the camper bounced along the dirt road. This was her first camping trip to Arizona. She was glad her cousin John and her Uncle Martin had asked her to go along and allowed her to bring Boomer.

"Are we almost there, Dad?" asked John.

"Almost," said Uncle Martin. He put his hand up to shade his eyes. The late afternoon sun was shining right in his face. "We'll be settled before night sets in," he said, adjusting the sun visor.

"Boomer's going to love the desert," said Patty.

The big German shepherd wagged his tail and sniffed the dusty air.

Uncle Martin turned off the road and parked the pickup near a sandy wash. They popped out the tent and set up camp. Everyone had a job to do. While they worked, Boomer ran all over, sniffing and pawing at rocks and checking out holes in the ground.

"Keep an eye on your dog, Patty," warned Uncle Martin. "If he takes off after a rabbit, he could get lost out here."

No sooner were the words spoken, than Boomer spotted a roadrunner and raced after it. Patty and John sprang after the dog, scrambling through scratchy bushes and around prickly pear cactus as they went.

"Ow!" cried John. He stumbled down, clutching his ankle.

"Are you hurt?" asked Patty.

"It's just a sprain. I stepped in a hole, I think. I'll be OK. You go get Boomer. I'll head back to the camper for some ice."

Patty could hear barking up ahead, but the dog was loping away faster. "Boomer! Come back here!" she yelled. Boomer kept on running.

There wasn't any trail to follow, so Patty concentrated on the direction of Boomer's barking. Twice she spotted the dog. He just glanced back at her and woofed, then he took off again. A lot of good those obedience classes were, Patty thought angrily.

She followed a sandy wash for a while, calling for Boomer every few minutes. Soon she realized she was in a canyon. Red stone walls loomed over her. Silence surrounded her. It was way too quiet. She heard no more barking. Nothing moved and the daylight was fading fast.

A small ledge caught her eye so she climbed up to get a better look. "BOOMER!" she yelled. This time she did hear something—an echo. Her own words came bouncing off the walls back to her. She tried not to let the panic bubbling up inside her take over. Stay calm, she told herself. Head back to camp. Maybe Boomer will come back on his own.

Then she gulped. Head back? Sure. But which way? Patty spun around, looking for any familiar marker. All she saw were sandstone walls and dry washes coming together in the canyon. Which sandy wash had led her here? By now, the sun had disappeared and long shadows had closed in on her from every side. If she tried to find her way out now, she might get even farther away from camp. She decided the best plan was to stay put and try to figure something out.

She hunkered down beside a boulder the size of a small car. It would protect her a little from the cold night air. Already, the chilly air was raising goose bumps on her arms. She tried not to think about having to stay there all alone. She longed for her warm bedroll back in the camper. Her stomach growled. She fumbled in her pocket and came up with a small package of crumbled oatmeal cookies. Some dinner!

As she nibbled on a cookie, she heard a rustling sound in the rocks nearby. She froze. Coyotes and mountain lions live in the desert she remembered. They like to hunt at night, too. She picked up a rock, ready to throw it at whatever was coming toward her. The shape moved closer. It looked like a wolf.

"Go away!" cried Patty, flinging the rock.

"Woof!" came the answer.

"Boomer! You scared me!" She threw her arms around his furry neck and was rewarded with slobbery dog kisses. "Boy, am I glad to see you!"

Patty gave Boomer one of the cookies and ate the rest herself. "At least we can keep each other warm tonight," she said. She looked up at the night sky filled with stars. They seemed so much brighter and closer here in the desert. She picked out her favorite constellation, Orion. With its three stars for a belt and four stars marking the arms and legs of the "Hunter," Orion was easy to spot.

"At least there's one familiar sight out here, Boomer. Remember how we would stand in our driveway at home and see Orion? Makes me feel like we're back there." Patty lay back, closed her eyes and thought about her house. At home she looked south to find Orion. Orion which always moved across the sky from east to west....

"Of course!" cried Patty, sitting up. "I know how we can find our way back. We were heading west, into the sun when we stopped. Remember how Uncle Martin had to shade his eyes? You ran off to the north, Boomer. That means we have to go east and south to find the camper."

The dog wagged his tail and started to pace.

"Come on, Boomer. Let's get out of here." Patty and her dog followed the wash that led southeast. Soon they were out in the open again. A full moon bathed the desert with its cool light.

Patty checked the stars again. Orion to the south. Big Dipper to the north. She continued heading southeast, Boomer at her side. Soon she heard voices shouting her name. Flashlights bobbed toward her.

"Uncle Martin! Here we are!" shouted Patty. Boomer barked and ran toward the lights.

"You two gave us quite a scare," said Uncle Martin when he caught up with Patty. "We didn't know which canyon you'd wandered into."

"Weren't you scared out there all alone?" asked her cousin John, handing her a bottle of water.

"We weren't completely alone," said Patty, pointing up to the sky. "Our friend Orion was with us."

SALT ON A BIRD'S TAIL

A folktale from Sweden

Once there was a boy named Olle who always wanted what he couldn't have.

"If only I had a shiny knife, I could carve toys to play with," Olle would say. "If only I had a wagon, I could carry my toys everywhere. If only I had a pony. . . ."

One day he saw a magpie in a tree. He had heard that if a person put salt on a magpie's tail, the bird had to grant the person's wishes.

All afternoon he chased after the bird until he was too tired to run anymore. Then the bird flew down and spoke to him.

"Are you looking for me?" she asked.

"You can talk!" cried Olle.

"Oh yes," said the bird. "You see, I'm really a princess with magic powers. And I'll let you put salt on my tail and make your wishes. But first you must do something for me."

"Anything!" said Olle.

"Bring me a shiny little knife so I can trim my claws. A princess must look neat."

Olle got busy picking berries in the forest and took them to town to sell. Soon he earned enough money to buy a knife. He put some salt in his pocket and hurried back to the forest.

But when the bird saw the knife, she laughed. "This is just a plain pocket-knife. I wanted one with a silver handle, fit for a princess."

"Then I will get you that kind," said Olle.

"No, never mind. Now I want a wagon to carry my things. A princess has lots of things, you know."

So Olle took the knife and carved toys for the children in town. He was a good carver, too. He made cows, horses, and birds. The children loved the toys and begged their mothers to buy them. Soon Olle had enough money to buy a wagon.

But when the magpie saw the wagon, she flapped her wings angrily.

"A princess can't use a wagon like that. I wanted one with gold trim and velvet cushions."

"Then I will get it for you," said Olle.

"No, never mind. Now I want a pony. A princess likes to ride in style."

So Olle took the wagon and ran errands for the people in town. He carried loads of wood one day and vegetables the next. He gave rides to everyone. Soon he had earned enough money to buy a handsome black pony. He was sure the bird would like it.

But when the magpie saw the black pony, she shook her head. "I really prefer brown ponies," she said.

The boy plopped down on the ground with a huff. "You are so hard to please," he said. "You wanted a knife, and I got you a knife. You wanted a wagon, and I got you a wagon. You wanted a pony, and here is a pony. If you are not happy, then I'll never get to put salt on your tail and make my wishes!"

"You're right," chirped the bird. "I am hard to please. But you have worked hard, and you have earned your wishes." She stuck out her tail and Olle sprinkled salt on it. "Now, tell me what you want," she said.

Eagerly, Olle said, "I want a . . . no, I have that. Then I want a . . . no, I have that, too."

"Hurry," said the bird. "Your time is running out!"

Olle suddenly realized something important. "I don't need you!" he said. "Now I know how to get the things I want without making wishes."

The bird laughed. "Imagine that!" she said. And away she flew.

THE PACK RAT PUZZLE

The sun beat down on Jesse's back as he bent over a little wire cage. He slowly opened the trap door, letting a furry creature run into the Arizona desert.

"Adiós, Number 12!" he shouted. Jesse secured the wire cage on his bike and headed back to Mrs. Bernson's house. Since he had started his job catching pack rats, he'd caught and released a dozen of the pesky rodents into the desert, away from houses.

He was soon back at work, tearing apart the

pack rat's nest from around the prickly pear cactus. If he left it there, a new pack rat might move in. He raked out sticks, bits of cholla cactus, and a few bottle caps. Pack rats love to pick up any scrap or shiny object and drag it home.

The nest was a huge mound, about two feet high and four feet across. As Jesse hoisted the last of the debris into the trash barrel, something metallic caught his eye. He picked up a tarnished silver bracelet with five little charms.

He touched each charm—a saguaro cactus, a hula dancer, a sail boat, a horse, and a disk with a piece of turquoise on one side and the date Dec. 15 on the other. Was it someone's birthday, or an anniversary? The bracelet must have been important to someone.

Jesse asked Mrs. Bernson if it was her charm bracelet, but she shook her head. "No, I've never liked them," she said. "Too jiggly for my taste."

"I'd like to find the person it belonged to and return it," Jesse said.

Mrs. Bernson thought for a moment. "We bought this house from the Murrays six years ago. They moved over to Sunrise Drive. I'll give you their address."

As he biked over to the Murrays' house, Jesse thought of a list of questions to ask about the bracelet. He didn't want to blurt out, "Did anyone ever lose a silver bracelet?" He had to be sure he was giving it to the rightful owner. The cactus charm fit the desert area, but what about the others? Solving a mystery would add some excitement to his job.

Jesse rang the bell, and an older man answered the door.

"Hullo, I'm Jesse Andrews. I was clearing pack rat nests over at your former house. I found something that might belong to someone in your family."

Mr. Murray arched his bushy eyebrows. "How interesting! What is it?"

"Well, first may I ask you some questions?"

"Sure. Fire away."

"Do you, or did you, own a sailboat?"

Mr. Murray nodded. "We used to. We took it over to San Diego on long weekends."

"Did you ever take your boat to Hawaii?" Jesse asked.

"No, but we flew there on vacation once."

"Did you own horses when you lived in that house?"

"No horses," said Mr. Murray. "My daughter loved to ride them, though."

"May I talk to her?"

Mr. Murray laughed. "You're quite the detective, aren't you? Susy lives up in Oregon now with kids of her own. Wait here and I'll get her on the phone for you."

He brought his cell phone to the porch and explained the situation to his daughter. Then he handed the phone to Jesse.

"Hi," Jesse said. "Sorry to bother you, but maybe you can help me solve a mystery."

"What fun!" said Susy. "I love a good mystery."

"Your dad says you used to go horseback riding," Jesse said.

"Yes. My friend Milena owned a couple of horses."

Jesse smiled, feeling he was getting closer.

"Would you mind telling me your birthday?"

"Sure. It's December fifteenth."

Jesse pumped his fist, certain that Susy was the owner. "I think I've found your silver charm bracelet."

"But I never owned one," said Susy.

"You didn't? But everything fits. All the charms match things from your life. There's even a disk with December 15 on the back."

Susy was quiet for a moment. "You know, my friend Milena, the one with the horses, she and I had the same birthday. We did everything together. I'd go riding with her, and she'd come sailing with us. She moved back to Hawaii, but we keep in touch by e-mail. I'll give you her address."

That night, Jesse placed the charm bracelet by his computer. After studying it, he sent a list of questions to Milena. The next morning he had an e-mail reply from her:

Hi Jesse—I think I know what you found. Susy and I celebrated a tenth birthday together at her house. Later I discovered that I'd lost my silver charm bracelet. We looked everywhere for it. It's been twenty years since that party! I'd forgotten all about it until I saw your list of questions. My bracelet had a horse for my palomino, a hula girl because I was from Hawaii, a saguaro for Arizona, and a sailboat because I love sailing. The turquoise is the birthstone for people born in December!

Jesse grinned as he typed a reply: *Mystery solved! I'll mail the bracelet to you today.*

A week later, he got another e-mail from Milena:

Thanks for the bracelet. What can I send you as a reward?

Jesse sent her a goofy request: *How about the ocean? It's still hot and dry here in Arizona.*

The next week a package arrived in the mail for Jesse. It wasn't the whole ocean, just little bits and pieces that smelled of sea salt and tropical breezes. Tucked inside a half coconut shell Jesse found some coral sand, a smooth piece of bottle glass, a sea shell and an orchid wrapped in a plastic bag. He smiled, wondering what that pack rat would have thought of these strange items that came from a place so far from the desert.

PALOMA

Based on a folktale from Spain

In a small dusty village, there lived a poor man with his beautiful daughter. He knew his life would soon end so he called her to his side for one last talk.

"I must send you away to find a better life for yourself," he said. He opened a large trunk and pulled out three splendid dresses. "These once belonged to your mother. I wish I had more to give you."

The first dress shimmered with golden suns. The second one glowed with silvery moons. And the third one sparkled with stars.

"Thank you, Father!" said the girl. "But how can I ever leave you?"

"You must go, my child. Somewhere, happiness awaits you."

With a heavy heart, the girl took the bundle of dresses and kissed her father goodbye.

Along the road she met an old woman wearing a shawl of dove feathers.

"Where are you going?" asked the woman.

"I'm looking for a place to stay," replied the girl. "Of course, I'm willing to work for my keep."

The old woman nodded in understanding. "Soon you will come to a great hacienda. The señora there will give you work." She took off her feathered shawl and wrapped it around the girl. "For now, cover your beauty and let your actions guide you. Someday you can reveal who you really are."

When the girl came to the hacicnda, she saw how neglected it was. Weeds choked the garden, the fountain sat silent and dry, and the windows of the house were dark and dreary.

The señora gave her a job as a servant. Feeling ashamed, the girl wouldn't give her real name. Instead, she said she was called Paloma, which meant 'dove.'

As Paloma did her chores, she learned why the

hacienda was so sad. The señora was a recent widow. She had sent away all her servants and was waiting for her son, Fernando, to come home.

Little by little, Paloma brought life back to the house. She cleaned the grime from the windows, letting in the bright sun. Roses, daisies, and honeysuckle blossomed in the garden. The old fountain bubbled with water again. Birds flocked to the garden, filling the air with song.

At last Fernando arrived. When Paloma served dinner that night, she noticed how handsome and intelligent he was. She felt a stirring of love grow in her heart.

"The hacienda looks beautiful," Fernando told his mother. "It will be a lovely setting for my wedding."

Stunned, his mother asked, "Who will you marry?"

"I don't know yet," said Fernando. "Let's invite all the young ladies from the area to a three day fiesta. I'm sure I can find one who will be my bride."

On the night of the first fiesta, lovely señoritas

and their parents mingled on the patio. Luminarias flickered along the walks as music from the mariachis filled the air. Paloma wished she could join them. But how could she, dressed in her old feather shawl? Then she remembered the dresses her father had given her. She ran to her room and put on the golden sun dress.

When Paloma stepped into the patio, she lit up the night. No one recognized her as the lowly maid. Fernando asked her for every dance. When the evening was over, he gave her a golden bracelet.

"Come again tomorrow night," he begged.

"I will," she promised.

The second night, Paloma wore the silvery moon dress. Once again, no one recognized her, and as before, Fernando danced only with her. When she started to leave, he gave her a pearl necklace.

"Promise you'll return tomorrow night!"

"I promise," she said .

The third night, Paloma arrived in her sparkling star dress. She and Fernando danced all night under the moonlit sky. When the music ended,

Fernando gave her a diamond ring.

"Take me to your father so I can ask for your hand."

Knowing she could not do that, Paloma hung her head. What would Fernando think if he knew she was only the maid? Ashamed of her deception, she ran away and hid in her room.

In the following days, Fernando rode to all the ranches looking for his mystery lady. When he couldn't find her, he became sad and ill. Paloma knew it was all her fault and that she must help him. She hurried to the kitchen and made up a kettle of squash blossom soup. She sent it out to him and he ate it all. In the bottom of the bowl he found the golden bracelet.

"Who made this soup?" he demanded.

Feeling jealous, his mother said, "It's from my own kitchen to make you well again."

The next day, Paloma sent Fernando a pot of green chile stew. In the bottom of his bowl he found the pearl necklace.

"Mother, who brought this stew?" he asked.

Again, his jealous mother only answered, "I'm

pleased you like it my son."

Next, Paloma made him a sweet golden custard. She watched from the shadows as Fernando ate carefully until he found the diamond ring. For a moment he sat there, thinking. Then he glanced her way, and rushed over to her.

"Don't be afraid, Paloma," he said, taking her hand. "You are the lady I've been seeking. You have brought life back to this house. You made me well again."

His mother cried out, "You cannot marry this poor beggar girl! She is only the maid!"

"No, she is much more," replied Fernando. "My princess is warm like the sun, gentle like the moon, and bright like the stars. Even a cloud of feathers cannot hide her from me."

Realizing she no longer had to hide or feel ashamed, Paloma dropped her feathery shawl and stood before him in her sparkling dress.

Fernando's great happiness softened his mother's heart. Three days later, Paloma and Fernando were married in one more grand fiesta.

GOLD AND SILVER AND COPPER

There once was a young man named Bo. He was as stubborn as an old tree stump. He lived in Sweden and made his living as a blacksmith, pounding out horseshoes and tools on his anvil. One day, Bo arrived with his wife in the small village of Torp. The villagers were glad to have him, for up until then, they had to travel twenty miles to find a blacksmith.

Bo wanted to buy some land so he could build a house and forge. He decided on a place known as Trollbacken. It had a nice hill in the middle of a field and the blacksmith figured that would be a good spot to live and work. The owners of the land thought the blacksmith would build in the field. When they heard he was going to build on the hill, they tried to warn him.

"Don't do it!" they said. "There's little folk living under that hill. They don't like it when human folk move in on top of them."

Bo laughed at the warning, saying, "I don't believe in fairy tales!"

And so the blacksmith and his wife started to build. Every day it seemed they lost a tool or a piece of lumber. The couple argued, accusing each other of being careless with things. Once, after Bo had spent all day building the chimney to the forge, the stones he had used tumbled down in a heap the next day.

The neighbors understood what was going on. "It's the little folk, the small trolls under the hill that are causing your troubles. Go build somewhere else. You'll be much better off."

Of course, the stubborn blacksmith ignored them again. Finally, in spite of all the delays, the house and forge were finished.

One night, as Bo and his wife were getting ready for bed, they heard clanging noises from outside. Bo lit a lantern and went out to see what it was.

How surprised he was to see all his hammers, nails, iron rods, buckets, and pliers scattered all over the yard.

"We're not leaving!" he shouted into the darkness.

"Ooooo-hooo!" came the reply.

"It's only an owl," said his wife.

"Ooooo-hooo!" once again.

The blacksmith ignored this warning, too, and went about the business of taking care of people's horses and wagons. He kept the forge burning night and day. His customers asked how it was going, and to every one he replied, "Just fine, thank you."

One day, Bo was asked to come do some work a farm many miles away. It meant he'd have to stay the night.

"Now don't you worry," he told his wife. "You'll be just fine while I'm gone."

But his wife wasn't so sure. That night she locked all the doors and windows and pulled the drapes tightly closed. Whatever went on outside would be no concern of hers.

Before going to bed, she decided to have one more cup of coffee. As she lifted her old kettle from the hearth, something snatched it out of her hand and sent it clattering across the floor.

She peered into the dark shadows of her kitchen and saw a hairy troll staring back at her. He was no bigger than a cat, with a long, crooked nose. Clumps of mossy hair sprouted between the warts covering his body.

"What do you want?" the frightened woman asked.

"Gold and silver and copper," the troll answered.

"You've come to the wrong house, then. The only gold here is my wedding ring, and you're not getting that!"

"Gold and silver and copper. Gold and silver and copper," sang the troll over and over. He danced around the room, knocking pots and pans and dishes to the floor.

"Get out of my house!" yelled the woman. But in the next moment, it was she who was out of the house, standing barefoot in the yard. She ran down the road and did not stop until she came to the church. There, she huddled in a cold corner until the pastor found her in the morning.

All through the night, a fire raged through the blacksmith's house and forge. The neighbors tried in vain to put out the stubborn flames of gold, silver, and copper.

The blacksmith returned home to find his house in ruins and his wife in tears.

"I'll not go back to that place!" she cried. "It's haunted!"

Bo didn't believe that. What he did believe was that he had finally met someone more stubborn than he was. His will was no match for a troll's. The blacksmith gave back the land, moved away and built somewhere else.

To this day no house has been built on the hill at Trollbacken. Some people say, when the moon is full, they've seen little trolls dancing in the ruins on the hill. And if you listen carefully, you can still hear them singing, "Gold and silver and copper" all night long.

AUTHOR'S NOTE:

Did you like these stories?. If you did, I hope you'll write a review on Amazon.com. Reviews help other readers decide to read the book. Thanks in advance!

Earlier versions of the following stories have been published in magazines or books. They are reprinted here with permission from the publishers:

"*The Message of the Coquí*," Guide, August.1992.

"*The Troll Wedding*," Stories from Highlights: The Extraordinary Bubble, 1995.

"*Puma Pays a Visit*," Stories from Highlights: The Extraordinary Bubble, 1995.

"*Cactus Coyote*," Stories from Highlights: Cactus Coyote, 1995.

"*Sausage Heaven*," Stories from Highlights: Cactus Coyote, 1995.

"*Treasure in the Desert*," Stories from Highlights: Annabel Lee, P.I., 1995.

"*Blind Ambition,*" Stories from Highlights: Hideaway Hollow, 1995.

"*Emergency Pilot,*" Stories from Highlights: Emergency Pilot, 1995.

"Alone Under the Stars," Stories from Highlights: Emergency Pilot, 1995.

"*The Kidnapped Pumpkins,*" Stories from Highlights: Megan's Tree, 1995.

"*Salt on a Bird's Tail,*" Highlights for Children, December 1996.

"*Lucia for Grandma,*" Highlights Plus, December 1997.

"*Whispers in the Night,*" Highlights Plus, June 1998.

"*Captain Purple,*" Pockets, October 1998.

"*Windows of Gold,*" Highlights for Children, Sept. 1999.

"*Gold & Silver & Copper,*" from *Over the Waves,* Rafter Five Press, August 1999.

"*The Pack-Rat Puzzle,*" Highlights for Children, December 2000.

Gullywasher Gulch, published by Boyds Mills Press, 2002.

ABOUT THE AUTHOR

Marianne Mitchell is the award-winning author of thirteen books for young readers and over 300 short stories and articles in national magazines, including *Highlights for Children, Highlights High Five, Pockets,* and *Jack and Jill.* She lives in Tucson, Arizona with her writer husband, Jim, and their two dogs. You can find her on the Web at www.MarianneMitchell.net.

67699411R00089

Made in the USA
Charleston, SC
19 February 2017